I0542793

The Desire To Control

The Complete Series

A BWWM BILLIONAIRE ROMANCE

Jaelynn McCranie

The Desire To Control/ Jaelynn McCranie -- 1st ed.
Xplicit Press, an imprint of TLM Media LLC

ISBN-13: 978-1-62327-645-4
ISBN-10: 1-62327-645-4
eISBN: 978-1-63497-047-1

Printed in the United States of America

CONTENTS

1

It was dark. Here she was blindfolded and tied to the four corners of the bed post like an animal waiting to be slaughtered. She heard movements in the room, and she could feel her heart pounding against her chest. She felt the bed sink, and she turned her head in that direction.

"I'm going to massage you with some oil now ok?"

She nodded. She felt his weight on her, straddling her. She could feel his bulge nestling into her warm flesh as he sat lightly on her tummy. He wasn't naked, though; she could feel the soft material of his boxers on her bare skin. Something inside of her wanted him to be naked, wanted him to not just sit on her but to fuck her, and fuck her hard. But she had to wait. This was his game, and she was just the pawn.

The smell of the oil lingered in her nostrils as he rubbed her arms slowly. It was a soft scent almost like lavender with a mix of vanilla. His touch was electric. Her nerves were on end just as it was the first day that they met. She heard stories about him, but never in her wildest dreams did she think she would become one of his fantasies. She tried not to respond to him, but her body was deceiving her; her pulsed raced, her breath ragged, and her pussy was already moist.

His hands explored her breasts, tugging gently at her nipples, squeezing them lightly in his hands. She felt something tight squeeze her nipples, and she cried out. The pain of the clamps shot right to her pussy. It felt good in a weird sort of way. If there was anything like good pain, this was it. Her stomach felt hot. The tip of his tongue passed over her nipples gently. He blew on them making her shiver. She was going through so many emotions; she felt as though she was going to explode. No man had ever made her feel like this, ever.

His body shifted as his hands ventured to her lower regions, careful not to touch her intimate areas just yet. Soft moans escaped from her parted lips as his hands lingered on her inner thighs before heading downward to her feet.

He took each of her toes into his mouth and sucked them. Shivers went up her spine. She squirmed as she could feel the heat rising from within her. The more she squirmed, the slower he went and the slower he went, the more aroused she became.

She held her breath as something tickled her skin. She wiggled her feet as it trailed higher up her legs, to her inner thighs. It continued to move higher as it circled her navel, then headed up to her full breasts. Her already swollen nipples hardened even more as to what seemed to be a feather circled one and then the other, causing the pain to intensify. She arched her breasts towards him, but instead of continuing he brushed his lips against hers.

The feather left her skin sensitized to

the touch, and her body ached and was hungry for more.

She heard the soft buzz of a motor. Her heart skipped a beat. She quivered with anticipation. She moaned softly as the vibrator touched her nipples lightly, teasing and taunting them. She was afraid to seem too eager in case he moved it away from her. Her breath became shorter, faster as between her legs throbbed with impatience. She began to sway slightly beneath him.

"You are an eager one aren't you?" he whispered huskily in her ears, his breath leaving heated trails on her skin.

She wanted to feel his lips on her, kissing, caressing her with his mouth. She wanted him to nibble her in her most intimate places and take her over the edge. Her moans became louder as the vibrator trailed her stomach slowly.

Her legs seemed to have a consciousness of their own as they opened, already dripping. Her pleasure increased as the vibrator lingered on her inner thighs.

"Ahhh," she groaned. She didn't know how long she would be able to contain herself. She began to wiggle impatiently.

"Please touch me," she begged.

"I want to see you cum."

She had no time to be shy. Masturbation wasn't unnatural to her, but she had never put on a show for anyone, not even Dean.

She shrieked with pleasure as the vibrator touched her clit. His hands opened her wet folds, giving him full access to her inner self. She lifted her hips and opened her legs as wide as she could.

"I love how wet you are. Now it's my turn to have some fun."

The buzzing was no more. He took off her blindfold. "I want to see those pretty eyes of yours." His eyes were filled with desire. His lips pressed against hers, and she responded to him hungrily. Every hormone in her body was raging by now.

"Fuck me, please," she whimpered like a puppy.

His hands glided themselves under her ass, and he directed his attention to her well-shaven pussy. He slid one finger into her, and his mouth covered her, his tongue circling her clit, his eyes still gazing into hers. She cried out again, pulling and tugging at the bondages that held her hands. He added more fingers and increased the stimulation to her clit. She was ready to go over the top.

"Oh shit, oh shit." She tried to wiggle free from his face, but he held her even closer. She wanted to cum but not all over him. She began to panic; she wiggled frantically. But the more she wiggled, the faster he rubbed her clit.

"I want you to cum. Let it go baby."

She couldn't hold it any longer. She screamed as she squirted over him. She felt exhausted as her body sank into the bed. His face never left her pussy as he licked up her juices hungrily.

"I'm not finished yet with you babe." He looked up at her and smiled. "We've only just begun."

2

"Come in, " came the gruff voice of Rick Forrest, President, and Founder of Forrest Empires, the largest real estate business, in the state.

Blake entered the office, and Rick waved his hand for him to sit in a chair, still focused on the phone conversation that he was having.

"I don't care how you get it done, just get it done!" Rick slammed the receiver down and rubbed his temples.

"Here are the files that you wanted," Rick said, handing over the Smith files to his father. Jovon Smith had been doing business with his father for years, but now that his daughter was taking over she was thinking about changing who they do business with.

Rick flipped through the files, making sure that everything was where it should be. He handed back the files to Blake, "Take these down to Ridge, he's having a meeting with Smith's daughter at 10 o'clock."

"But.I thought that you were giving me this case?" Blake said, his blue eyes glaring. This would have been his chance to prove himself to his father.

"This is too much of a big deal Blake. We can't afford to blow this."

The phone rang again, and Blake knew that the conversation was over. Blake left his father's office and headed toward the elevators. He was lucky enough to get an empty one. He wasn't in the mood to rub shoulders with anyone today.

Being tall, blonde and rich made him a "catch" with the ladies. There was never a woman that he wanted that he could not have. They were putty in his hands, willing to obey every command that came from his lips. Blake knew how to command respect from the opposite sex only if it were that simple to command respect from Rick Forrest.

The elevator bell rang indicating that he had reached his destination. He walked over to Ridge's secretary and handed her the documents. Just then Ridge's office door opened.

"Hey there, Blake."

Blake nodded before turning to walk away. If he heard one smug remark from Ridge, he would have punched him right there and then. This time, he wasn't alone in the elevators.

"Hi, Blake."

"Hi, Andrea."

Andrea was his new plaything at the office. They would usually steer clear of each other during work hours. Maybe this was a sign.

"Sorry about the Smith case."

Blake looked at her. It never ceased to amaze him at how fast bad news got around in their twenty story office building. He looked over at Andrea. Her black, shoulder-length hair was pulled back in a tight bun, her skirt was two inches too short, and the first two buttons of her blouse were undone, showing her full breasts. It took everything in him not to take her right there and then.

As though reading his mind, she asked: "Is there anything I can do to help?"

"As a matter of fact, there is." Blake stopped the elevator and pressed his body firmly against Andrea's, against his better judgment.

"You smell nice," he said as he tasted her neck. His hands moved to hurriedly lift her skirt over her hips. He smiled as he entered her with his fingers. Andrea wasn't big on wearing underwear, which made it all the easier for him. He nuzzled her neck as he enjoyed the warmth of her. Blake quickly pulled out his hard cock and thrust it into her, hard.

She moaned loudly and held on to his shoulders as he thrust into her repeatedly.

"Yes, Blake," she moaned, her hands running through his hair.

She felt tight around his cock. He hoisted her up, and she wrapped her legs around his waist causing her skirt to rise to her waist. He pinned her against the elevator wall. They didn't have the whole day he needed to get this extra tension out of his system, now! He was happy that his father didn't install the cameras in here, or he would be screwed. He exploded inside her and slowly set her on her feet. They quickly adjusted their clothing and Blake started back the elevator, both appearing as though nothing had happened.

The elevator doors opened, and she stepped out without another word swaying her hips as she walked away.

Blake finally reached Henry Montgomery's office. His secretary gave him a pleasant smile as she waved him in. He opened the door and saw Monty eating a hamburger, fries and drinking a chocolate milkshake.

"Jill would have a fit if she saw you." Blake smiled, sitting in the empty chair opposite Monty's massive mahogany desk.

With silver highlights by his black hairline, apart from his rounding middle Monty looked nothing like his 65 years of age. Blake had never known life without Monty.

"She would only know if someone in here tells her and that someone is not going to be me." He sniffed the air playfully. "Do I smell a snitch in the room?"

"That all depends," Blake said, playing along. "Is there another burger there for me?"

Monty opened his desk drawer and handed Blake a brown paper bag. "There you go. Sorry about the shake, though," he said nodding his head towards the bin, "it's been a rough morning."

Blake took out the hamburger and took a huge bite. He woke up late this morning, and he didn't have time to eat breakfast. So far he was working on a stomach full of coffee.

"I heard about the Smith case," Monty said, finishing off his shake and tossing it into the bin.

"Yeah, yeah story of my life. I don't even know why I bother," Blake said with a mouth full of fries.

"If you want me to talk to him I will."

"Nah, I'm good. I just can't stand the fact that he didn't even consult me before giving it to Ridge. I'm just as good as Ridge or even better in my opinion, but that man just wouldn't give me a chance."

"You have to demand it with Rick. I know you are one of the best that we have here, but you have to stand firm with him. Make him see you. Don't back down. I have a case here that you should do great with." Monty handed him the case file. Blake put it aside. He'd read it once he got back to his office.

Monty looked at him mischievously, "Ok, so let's get off the topic of work for one minute and tell me about that hot blonde I saw you with last night."

****

Cassie knocked on the door of the Parker's apartment. Today was the 15th. They asked her if she could give them a little more time because Mr. Parker had just been laid off.

A pregnant, Mrs. Parker opened the door with a two-year-old, Amy clutching tightly at her mother's skirt. She moved out of the way so that Cassie could enter.

Even though the apartment was small, it was neat and homey. Everything didn't look new, but they made the best of what they had.

"Would you like a cup of tea?"

"Sure."

"I'm waiting for Paul to come back. I'm hoping he has some good news." Mrs. Parker set two steaming cups of brewing tea on the small kitchen table before setting the cream and sugar on the table as well.

After a few minutes of catching up with Mrs. Parker and her pregnancy, Paul came through the door. He was a bit taken aback by seeing Cassie, but he smiled anyway. He kissed his wife and his baby girl, who was glad to see him. He lifted her in his arms before sitting by the table. Cassie couldn't help but wonder if one day someone would come home to her and kiss her as passionately as Mr. Parker kissed his wife.

Mr. Parker turned to Cassie. "I'm sorry Ms. Wells. I don't have the money for you today as I was hoping, but I did get a job down at the gas station. It doesn't pay much, but at least, it's a start."

"Praise God," his wife said happily with tears streaming down her face as she looked over at her husband.

"That is great news, Mr. Parker. When you have the money, give me a call, and I'll pass and collect it." Cassie left the apartment leaving the Parkers to celebrate Mr. Parker's new job.

Cassie walked down the five flights of stairs to get to the apartment that she had grown up in with her parents and her sister, Samantha. When Sam called her to tell her about their father, she didn't believe that things were this bad.

Her father was diagnosed with cancer and being the proud man that he was, kept it to himself until he was so bad that Sam had to go with him to the emergency room, and that was when they found out. Her father was still talking and moving about but spent most days in bed resting.

Cassie couldn't remember ever seeing her father asleep during the day as a child. She always knew her father to be a great man and provider for their family. She hoped that one day she could be as lucky as her mother was.

The love that she felt for her parents was somewhat magical. She always wondered why her father never remarried after her mother passed away. Maybe he couldn't find someone else to fill that special place.

Cassie opened the door gently to the apartment, hoping not to wake her father in case he was resting. She headed straight for the small office at the back of the apartment where her father usually sat when everyone was in bed.

"Dad?" Cassie said, surprised to see her father sitting behind the desk with a few files in front of him.

"Hi honey," her father said, looking up at her with a smile.

"What are you doing? You are supposed to be resting." She moved towards him and planted a kiss on his cheek.

"I can only rest for so long, Cassie. A man needs to provide for his family."

Cassie took her father's hand in his, "Daddy, you've taken care of us for long enough, it's time that we took care of you. How about you head to bed and I'll come in a bit and watch one of those old Bruce Lee movies with you?"

Cassie watched as her father's eyes lit up. She helped him get up from the office chair, and she steered him toward the door. She felt her eyes swell up with tears as she watched her father walk slowly towards his bedroom. Cancer took so much out of him. Her mother always said that her father was all the coffee he needed, tall, strong and black, but now he looked fragile and weak.

She tried to neaten the desk before

attending to her father when one piece of paper caught her eye with the name Rick Forrest. She would look into it some more after she got her father settled and he was resting. But for now, she was going to enjoy the movie that her father loved. She took off the light and headed towards her father's bedroom.

3

Blake walked into the conference as confident as usual. Thanks to Monty he already knew that the meeting was about, and he was a step ahead his colleagues. He nodded as he entered the room and took his seat. The conference room slowly began to fill and soon there was chatting and laughter in the air as they waited for Rick and Monty to arrive.

As soon as they arrived the room became silent. His father took his seat at the head of the table, and Monty sat at his right side. The pair looked grim.

"Ok, let's get down to business. The Wilkins, one of our biggest clients, would like to construct with our help, of course, a hotel. The only requirement for the hotel is that it must be close to the waterfront."

"But there isn't any space available by the waterfront," Ridge interrupted.

"There is always space by the waterfront," Blake said smoothly. "You just need to know where to look."

Rick continued, "The property that they are looking at buying is the old Well's Motel. Everything around it has changed, and the Wilkins' think that the new hotel could bring some revenue into the community and a few jobs as well. However, Mr. Wells is a very stubborn man. I've been trying to get him to sell that property now for over ten years."

Monty looked directly at Blake, "We need someone who can seal the deal."

"The person chosen for this task will have a maximum of three months to sell the property," Rick said with an edge in his voice. "People, we can't afford to lose this client."

"And you won't." Ridge jumped out of his chair adjusting his three-piece suit, "Give me two months and I'll have that deal signed and sealed."

Blake stood up. "After ten years of trying to get this property from Mr. Wells, we need to have a solid plan. We need to make them an offer that they can't refuse, and that's where I come in."

Ridge laughed. "It would be your department if Mr. Wells was slim and curved in all the right places. After that big mess that you made with the Johnson's account, it's a wonder that you can still even call yourself an agent."

"Now look here…" Blake growled.

"Boys, boys…," Monty jumped in, "This is not going to solve anything."

"Monty is right, and we do need the best that we have working on this case."

Blake watched as his father looked at Monty, who shook his head.

Rick let out an audible sigh, "Ok Blake I'll let you take the lead on this one if at any time I feel as though you can't handle it, I'm giving it to Ridge."

Ridge had the smuggest look on his face that made Blake want to smack him. Calm down, Blake, you'll get your opportunity.

Rick walked out of the room,

followed by Monty showing that the meeting had been concluded.

As Blake passed by Ridge to exit the conference room Ridge said in a soft, menacing tone, "As soon as you mess up I'll be there to take over like I always do. You're lucky that you are still working for daddy."

Blake clenched his teeth and walked out the conference room without another word.

****

"Sam, what are we going to do about daddy's medical bills? Even though he's resting at home, the medication and treatments are still a bundle."

Cassie heard Sam sigh on the other end of the phone. For the past hour, they have been trying to figure out how they were going to make the renovations on the motel that was falling apart piece by piece and take care of their father. Even if they combined their savings, it wouldn't cover half the cost.

"What about if we raise the rent? I don't know when was the last time daddy did that," Sam suggested.

"We can't do that, Sam. Some of our tenants are already finding it hard to pay the rent that they have." Thoughts of the Parkers floated across her mind.

"What about..." Just then her intercom went on. It was Mack.

"Ms. Wells, there is a gentleman here by the name of Blake Forrest, who would like to have a word with you."

"Ok Mack, send him in." Mack was the maintenance man. He had worked with her father for over thirty years. She knew that she could trust Mack with her life as well as that of her father. When she was in the office, he would usually watch the front desk for her.

"I have to go Sam; we'll talk about this later." After getting confirmation from her sister Sam, she hung up.

Cassie found the time to read the paper that her father left on the desk with Rick Forrest's name on it. He had been trying to buy the property from her father for quite a while. She also read up on his son, Blake Forrest, who seemed to be the highlight of every party and changed women as often as he changed his socks. Cassie detested men like him to her core. She knew he was here to continue the work of his father. Cassie was just as stubborn as her father, or so her mother said, and she wasn't going to give Blake Forrest the satisfaction of walking away with the deed in his hand.

There was a knock at the door, and Cassie got up to open it.

Standing before her was a tall, broad-shouldered blonde with the most amazing eyes she had ever seen. Even with her 5'6 frame, she still felt overpowered by this man. His pictures didn't do any justice to him at all.

"Hello, how may I help you?" Cassie said in her most businesslike voice.

He extended his hand towards her, "Hi, my name is Blake Forrest. I'm here to speak to you about the motel."

"The infamous Blake Forrest, I know who you are. My name is Cassandra Wells. Come on in." She shook his hand firmly to let him know that she meant business.

"Have a seat Mr. Forrest. How can I assist you?" Cassie took her seat at her desk and Blake sat opposite her.

"Please call me Blake," he said, flashing one of his dazzling smiles.

"What is it about my father's motel

that you would like to discuss, Mr. Forrest?" She stressed as she showed him to a chair and she sat behind her desk. Damn, he was cute. She wouldn't mind running her fingers through his wavy hair, though. She always loved her men tall and dark, but if he tried she could be persuaded to change her preference.

"I would prefer to speak to Mr. Wells about this since this is his business." There was something about his eyes that mesmerized her. She needed to snap out of it, her father's motel was on the line. Remember Cassie, he is the enemy, and you detest guys like that.

"My father is ill at this time," Cassie said, trying to hold back the tears and stop her voice from breaking. This was the first person other than Sam that she had ever admitted to that her father was sick. "I will be handling all his business from now on," she said, clearing her throat. Was that concern on his face? His facial expression changed so quickly that she couldn't be sure.

"Well then, can I call you Cassandra?" he asked, leaning forward a bit in his chair.

"Ms. Wells will be fine." His eyes danced with amusement.

"Ok. Ms. Wells," he stressed her last name just as she did with his. "Forrest Empires is going to purchase this property," he said, in a matter of fact kind of voice.

"We are not selling. It has sentimental value to all of us. What makes you think that you can just waltz in here and tell me that you are going to purchase this property?" Cassie said, through gritted teeth.

She watched as Mr. Forrest pulled out a piece of paper from his briefcase and slid it onto the table.

"The owner of this property is Bob Jones. His brother, Raymond Jones, sold this property to your father, but it wasn't his to sell. I tried contacting Mr. Jones, but he has passed away."

Mr. Forrest handed over the death certificate was well as a copy of the will. Their fingers touch and Cassie pulled away her hand a bit too quickly knocking over a glass of water that she was drinking earlier.

"Oh, crap." She stood up quickly as she grabbed a few tissues from the box on her table and began to wipe up the water before it spread all over the table.

For a tall guy, Mr. Forrest moved quite quickly because he was standing next to her trying to get the papers out of the way before they got wet. She wondered if he knew how close he was standing to her, or furthermore the effect that he was having on her. Even though she knew about his reputation she couldn't help but wonder how it would feel to be in his arms.

"Ms. Wells?"

Cassie looked up to see Blake staring at her with those deep blue eyes of his. She felt conscious about the top that she was wearing now that exposed her cleavage, but it would seem too childish if she threw her sweater on, after all, they are both adults.

"Um, yes?" Damn, she wanted those lips of his on her. She had to admit that he was stirring feelings inside her, and she wasn't sure if it was because she hadn't gotten laid in a while or it was because of who he is and his reputation. In the business world, the Forrest name meant power and the name Blake meant the same thing in the bedroom.

"I was asking if you have everything under control here."

"Yes, thanks for your help. I could be a bit clumsy at times," she murmured. Yeah clumsy when I'm around handsome men.

He passed behind her lightly, touching her as he passed. There it was again that fluttering in her stomach. Who was she kidding? Blake Forrest didn't date girls like her and even if he did, what would they do together? They were from two different worlds.

"As I was saying," he said as he took his seat, "his daughter, however, is willing to sell the property. You have two months to vacate the premises."

She sat and stared at him. She felt as though someone just dropped a load of bricks on her chest. "So that's it? You just come in here and demand that we leave, and you think that's what we are going to do? How do I even know if these papers are real?" she said, looking at him squarely in the eyes to which he returned her gaze.

She felt as though his eyes were looking into her soul. As angry as she was at this man she couldn't help but notice the strength of his jaw line and how she would love to run her fingers along it and how good he looked in his well-tailored suit. Keep it together Cassie, this is business.

"I can assure you, Ms. Wells, every piece of documentation is real," he said in a calm voice.

"Where are all these people supposed to go? They are already struggling as it is." She heard her voice get louder.

"And apparently so are you," he said as he looked around the office at its peeling walls. "The documentation is all there. This is business Ms. Wells where the people are relocated really isn't my problem."

He stood up to leave and Cassie stood up as well. She headed to the door, hoping to keep him in a bit longer to discuss the matter.

"This isn't over Mr. Forrest. We are going to fight this," she said, with a lot more confidence than she felt. Who was she kidding? They didn't have money to pay a lawyer to look over the documentation. She had no doubt in her mind that all the papers that he provided were authentic.

"You are free to fight, but rest assured that you will lose. We are willing to give you some compensation for the number of years that you have been here, but in two months everyone needs to be cleared out." He moved a step closer to her closing the gap between them.

Cassie couldn't see herself taking the money and relocating while the other tenants were left homeless? They had nowhere to go. Some tenants like Mrs. Henry had lived there for most of her adult life. Most days she just sat outside by the balcony looking out, but no one came to visit her in years. How was she going to throw her out?

"Two months isn't going to be enough time for our tenants to find a new place and start over. I don't think that it would be the best thing for my father either to remove him from things that he is acquainted with." Cassie thought that if they were to just give in now, he father would be devastated, and all the fight that he has would be lost, and this move would send him to an early grave. "What if we were able to raise the money on our own would we be able to save the motel?"

"You really think that you could raise five million dollars in two months?" Mr. Forrest laughed.

Cassie was furious, "We sure as hell could try."

"Please note Ms. Wells," his tongue seemed to caress her name. "I always get what I want." He looked her over with a smile at the edge of his mouth. What did he mean by that? To make his point clearer, he stepped closer to her. This time, close enough for her to smell the faint scent of his cologne. He looked down at her, and she held her breath.

"I have a lot at stake in this deal," he said softly. "And I don't lose, ever." For a minute, she thought that he was going to touch her, but something stopped him. It was a good thing too because she was sure that right there and then she would have allowed him to. She really needed to get laid. Here this man had waltzed in here trying to take her father's motel, and she was wondering how big his cock was.

"We still have two months, so this isn't yours yet. So if you would excuse me, I have work to do."

Cassie stepped aside and opened the

door for Mr. Forrest, who walked out the office without another word. Cassie closed the door and walked slowly back to her chair. She buried her head in her hands and had herself a good long cry.

4

Blake watched in amusement as a well put-together Cassandra Wells stood before him. No woman had ever dared to just arrive at his home unannounced. This was his sanctuary. But he was curious to know the reason for her visit. No doubt that it would be about her father's motel.

"Thank you, Albert. Please make sure that we are not disturbed." Albert nodded and closed the door of Blake's office.

"What brings you here Ms. Wells, and at such a late hour?" He looked at the grandfather clock sitting opposite his desk. It was almost 10 o'clock.

She stood just as confidently as she

had in her office, her gaze fixed on him. Tonight she was wearing a black fitted dress that rounded her hips and showed her small waist. The low v neck of her dress showed the full swell of her breasts. Her long, black hair flowed gently over her shoulders. It made her look younger than the bun she had in her hair when they first met. He also noticed how flawless her skin was.

He pointed to the sofa where she took her seat; the dress inched up her long legs, exposing her thighs to him.

"Would you like something to drink?" Before she could answer, he walked towards his mini bar and poured her a glass of wine while he poured himself some whiskey. He handed her the wine and took his glass as he returned to his seat behind his desk.

"Well to answer your question. I just came from a function on behalf of my father, and I decided that since I was in the area that I would see if we could talk about the motel."

She took a sip of her wine and looked at him with her big brown eyes. Her fingers wrapped tightly around the glass. He hadn't heard about any function in this area. He wondered if she just got dressed up and decided to pay him a visit hoping that her feminine wiles might sway him. He must say he liked her approach.

"I'm sorry that you wasted a trip. There is nothing that I can do. It's out of my hands." His eyes never left hers.

"What do you mean it's out of your hands?" She glared at him. There it was again, that fire in her eyes. No woman had ever stood up to him before, and he could feel himself getting aroused.

"Sorry doll, but that's the way business is. You win some; you lose some."

"So that's your final answer? You win some; you lose some? What about all the people that are going to be homeless? There are young children as well as elderly folk in that motel and two months is not going to be enough." Her tone softened. She seemed somewhat genuinely concerned for the other tenants, which was admirable.

"Why do you care so much about them?" He took a sip from his glass.

"What do you mean?" she sounded confused.

"They're just tenants."

The Forrest Empire had evicted many people in their day and never had one landlord ever come to ask for extra time for the sake of their tenants. Cassandra Wells, however, there was something different about her.

"They are more than just tenants they are like family. Many of them have been living there for over ten years." She looked down into her glass. This was the first time that she didn't meet his gaze. "I'm also afraid that if I move my father that it would have an adverse effect on his health, and I'm not ready to lose my father just yet."

"So Ms. Wells what do you have to offer me? Maybe I can sway my father to find another waterfront view, but my father is not an easy man to persuade."

"Excuse me?"

"What are you willing to give up so that your father can live out the rest of his years in his motel?"

"If you are suggesting that I just fall into bed with you to help save my father you are mistaken. I am not that kind of woman." He watched as she gulped down the rest of her wine and placed the glass on the coffee table nearest to her nervously.

Blake couldn't believe his ears. He would be lying if he said he didn't have thoughts about how her flesh would feel under his but he would never "force" a woman, no matter the circumstances, to have sex with him. "That thought never crossed my mind, but since you did bring it up…." Blake watched her, his eyes intense. She twitched under his gaze.

"Ms. Wells. You can submit to me and save your father and the motel, or you can walk away and raise the five million dollars on your own. It's your choice."

"What do you mean by submit?" She looked at him curiously.

"It means that for one night you give yourself totally over to me. You do as I say no questions asked."

Cassie had a new fire in her eyes, "Fine, I'll play your little game, but first I would need a letter from you stating that all debt has been paid which would allow us to keep the motel and allow the tenants to keep their homes."

"You drive a hard bargain, Ms. Wells."

"Well, this is a business deal isn't it?" she said as a smile touched the soft corners of her mouth.

Blake couldn't help but smile. What was it about her that made her so irresistible? Even now it took everything in him not pounce on her.

"Indeed, it is. I'll send a car to pick you up tomorrow at 8 pm. I would have the paperwork completed by then."

He got up and walked her to his office door. "Albert will show you out. It was a pleasure doing business with you Ms. Wells."

Cassie nodded before exiting the office.

****

Cassie looked at herself in the mirror. She had to admit that she was a bit nervous because she didn't know what to expect tonight from Mr. Forrest. She chose a white dress that she bought a month ago. The top was tied behind her neck, it fitted to her waist, then flowed to just above her knees. She added a bit of eye shadow and some lip gloss. No jewelry required since she really wasn't going on a date.

"Don't you look pretty?" Sam said, eyeing her suspiciously.

Cassie jumped as her thoughts were interrupted.

"So who is he?" Sam asked, plopping herself down on Cassie's bed.

"Umm...it's no one really. Just a business...date." Cassie knew that she couldn't look Sam in her eyes because Sam always knew when she was lying.

"What will they be serving? Cassie-a-la-platter?"

Cassie laughed nervously and turned to Sam. "So is it a crime for a sister to want to look her best?"

"Of course not, but it would have been nice if you were actually going on a date. It has been three years Cassie; maybe it is time that you get back out there."

Yes, it had been three years, and the pain seemed as though it was yesterday. She cleared her throat, hoping it would stop the tears from welling in her eyes.

"I'll get back out there when the time is right." She looked down at her watch; 7:55- she wanted to be out there and waiting so that Sam wouldn't ask any more questions than she was already asking. "I've got to go. Don't forget to give dad his medication at nine ok?" She picked up her purse.

"Bye Cassie enjoy your business date," Sam said in a playful tone. Cassie laughed and walked outside to wait for the car.

Butterflies were doing cartwheels and somersaults in Cassie's stomach as she walked up the third flight of stairs. The last time she was with a guy was three years ago. Damn! If she knew she was going to be exercising, she would have bought her running shoes. The driver dropped her off and told her where to go and sped off. The places seemed to be deserted and not as luxurious as she thought it would be. She finally reached her destination, and she knocked on the door.

Blake arrived at the door with a robe on and a towel around his neck. Cassie couldn't help but feel hot all over. Her words caught in her voice, and she found herself staring at him.

"Good evening Cassandra." He smiled as he moved so she could enter the apartment.

"Good evening Mr. Forrest," Cassie said her mouth feeling dry.

"Tonight may be to close a business

deal, but it will be a night of fun, so you can call me Blake."

Cassie nodded as she looked around the apartment. Not only was it roomy but it had a modern and sophisticated touch to it.

"You seem surprised," he chuckled.

"More like exhausted. No elevator in the building?"

"Exhausted already?" he said with a twinkle in his eye, "but we haven't even started. No, there isn't an elevator. I like the exercise. Would you like something to drink?"

"Sure," Cassie said as she took a seat on the huge sofa and crossed her legs.

Blake handed her a drink and picked up the envelope that was on the coffee table.

"Here is the document that you asked for."

Cassie took the document and read it through carefully. Everything seemed legit. Maybe she should grab the document and make a run for it. She was on the track team in college; maybe she could outrun Blake.

"Excuse me?" she asked. Blake had asked her something.

"Is it ok?"

"Yes, it's fine."

"Then shall we sign it and get on with tonight's festivities?"

Tonight's festivities? Where did he think he was at an amusement park? She watched as Blake signed it, and then she did the same.

"Ok, now that that is over, let's take this to the next room. M'lady…" Blake extended his hand towards Cassie, which she took. Together they walked towards what seemed to be the bedroom door. She couldn't help but wonder what awaited her in that room.

5

Still shuddering from her last climax, she watched as Blake gently untied her arms and her legs. Then he removed the clamps that were on her breasts. She was dripping with sweat, and the sheet felt cold. She was too tired to even rub her wrist and her ankles where they hurt. As tired as she was, she felt euphoric. Nothing could have prepared her for the satisfaction that she received nor the constant craving that she now has for Blake Forrest.

She watched as he gently massaged her wrists, kissing them ever so softly with his lips before moving to her ankles. Her body was being reenergized by his touch. He looked at her, and she saw the animalistic desire for her flesh in his eyes. Her pussy still craved his massive cock. He stood up and held out his hand, which she took. He led her to another door. He opened it, and she could feel the rush of the cool breeze on her skin, and she shivered. She stepped outside and there was another bed and a small nightstand next to it.

She looked at him quizzically. "Are you serious?"

"As serious as a heart attack," he said, before capturing his lips with hers and kissing her fiercely. When he did release her lips, she found it hard to find the right words.

"But what if someone sees us?"

"Well, that is the whole thrill of it, isn't it? It's all about the adrenaline rush, my love."

He guided her to the bed and captured her mouth once more with his. His kiss was hard, full of desire and want. He eased her gently on the bed, their lips never parting. His fingers made their way once more to her pussy. Finding her entrance, he gently glided them in while his thumb found her clit.

She gasped softly as she clung to his shoulders. Her body began to fill once again with an intense sensation of longing. She wanted him in her. She wanted him to fuck her till she couldn't move, till she couldn't think. She tried to shift her body underneath him so that she could feel his cock on her, but he held her captive by the weight of his body.

"Please," she begged, "I need you in me."

He removed his fingers from within her and passed it gently across her lips. She licked her lips, tasting herself. He quickly removed his boxers and when he did Cassie knew he meant business. She had had a few boyfriends before but never had she seen a cock as large as his. She wondered if she could take it all.

"I...I.," she stuttered.

He pressed his fingers on her lips, "Don't worry, I'll go gently on you... for now."

He bent her knees, "Hold them," his voice was authoritative. She held with without saying another word. He quickly opened the drawer to the nightstand. Cassie heard a foil packet open.

She watched as he kneeled in front of her. She bit her lips as she felt his cock gliding up and down her pussy lips. She felt his fingers parting her and then the pinch of his cock entering her tight pussy.

She moaned with every inch of his cock that penetrated her.

"Relax baby," he said in a husky voice.

Cassie forced herself to do as he said. The burning intensified, and she squeezed her eyes together.

"Are you ok?" his voice almost in a whisper.

Cassie nodded. She knew once his cock was all the way in it would get better and she would ride that motherfucker all the way home.

Blake groaned as Cassie felt the last of him deep with her. He stayed there for a bit rotating his hips against her before pulling back out again. He held on to her feet as his cock went in and out of her causing her to lose sense of all reality. No longer did she care that they might be seen. She no longer cared that after tonight he may be in the arms of another woman. Nothing else mattered only what was happening now and she sure as hell was going to enjoy every minute of it.

It had been three years since a cock pleasured her. Yeah, she had a dildo but nothing compared to this. Blake Forrest was all man and maybe he was mixed with a little beast as well. He lowered her legs and leaned forward, thrusting his cock deeper into her.

"Oh fuck," Cassie screamed out. She wrapped his legs around his waist unconsciously wanting him nearer to her; to feel his weight on her, to kiss his lips, to bond with his masculinity. He dove into her again and again. She closed her eyes, and she listened to his groans and breathing as well as her own.

He nibbled her ear, her neck, and then he went down to suck her sore nipples. It was as though he couldn't get enough of her. His hands were groping, and his tongue was teasing her. Shivers of pleasure ran through her. She dug her fingers into his back as she rocked her hips against his matching his rhythm.

She could feel herself on the verge or

extreme explosion. But she didn't want it to end. She didn't want to go back home to her cold bed. She wanted to stay here in his arms, in his bed, in his life.

Blake groaned loudly as he poured himself into her which sent her on her own climax. Both breathless Blake fell down beside her. Both silent for a minute taking in all that had happened.

"Are you ok?" He looked over at her. Was that concern in his eyes? The big, bad Blake Forrest is showing concern for someone he had a "business" deal with?

Cassie smiled, "Yes, I'm ok." She was back to reality, "Are we done here?" He nodded and even though every muscle in her resisted Cassie got up, got dressed and left the building.

6

"What's wrong?" Sam looked at her strangely.

"I already told you, I'm ok." Cassie forced a smile as she shuffled some papers around on her desk.

It had been an entire month since she had had her "business meeting" with Blake. She felt like such an idiot. She was in such a hurry to get away from him that she had forgotten the papers. What if he didn't uphold his side of the deal after all; she had no proof that the property still belonged to them. What was she going to tell the tenants? What was she going to tell her father?

She still didn't tell Sam about Blake coming to evict them from the motel. If she did, then she would have a few other things to explain, such as how she was able to persuade the "Mighty" Blake Forrest not to evict them, and she didn't want to travel down that road anytime soon.

Her father's health was deteriorating fast, even with the chemo and the doctors said that there was nothing else they could do for him. They suggested that they put him in a hospice, but Sam and Cassie both agreed that it would be better if their father stayed at home to be around people who loved him. They were getting excellent support from their tenants, who would take turns taking care of him in shifts so that Cassie could get some rest. Sam wanted to help too, but Cassie insisted that she concentrate on her finals; this was her last year and now wasn't the time to get sidetracked. Sam protested but eventually Cassie was able to convince her that this was the best thing for her.

"Don't lie to me Cassie, I know that with daddy being ill, you are under pressure but there is more to it than that. I just wish that you would open up to me."

"You want me to open up? Dad is not ill; he's dying!!!! He's not getting over this. He's not going to one day get off his bed and come back behind his desk as he used to- he's DYING Sam. You want me to open up?" Cassie screamed," I have my Masters in Business, I should be working in a prestigious firm by now, but no, once again, II have to sacrifice my dreams for this family and when I thought I had found a little piece of happiness he was already married with his own family. I'm open now, are you happy?"

She grabbed her handbag and quickly retreated from the office, tears streaming down her face. She gave Mack a quick wave as she headed to the front door. She had no doubt in her mind that he heard everything she said. She didn't mean to get so upset, but she had been too strong for too long, and she was tired.

Thank goodness she never locked her car during the day. Her hands were shaking as she opened the door and sat behind the wheel. She frantically looked in her handbag for her keys. In frustration, she emptied all the contents of her purse onto the passenger seat. She grabbed the key and started the car. She needs to find somewhere to clear her head.

****

"Dammit, Blake this was where you were supposed to show me that you are the best man for the job. And here you go and pull a stunt like this." His father slammed his hands on his desk.

"I am the best man for the job. Just because the deal didn't go as you planned doesn't mean that it didn't work." Ridge paid Mr. Jones' daughter from his own finances, and he was able to buy out another property by the waterfront which the Wilkins approved.

"When I ask you to do something, I expect you to do it exactly how I asked you to," his father fumed.

"Oh, so now I get it. As long as we are all slaves to what you do then you are ok with it? What about taking initiative and thinking for ourselves? Or do you believe that you built this company on your own strength? No wonder mother left you."

Blake saw the hurt in his father's eyes, but he didn't care. He turned his back and walked out of his father's office. He knew it was a low blow, but he was tired of his father always telling him how everything should be done. He had a mind of his own, and he would be damned if he didn't start to make some choices of his own.

He headed straight to his office and told his secretary, Mrs. Humphrey, that he did not want to be disturbed for the rest of the day. He took off his jacket and adjusted it behind his chair, then sat behind his desk and opened his desk drawer.

He watched the envelope. He had been surprised when he saw it still on the table when Cassandra left. What surprised him even more was that she hasn't called him to collect it. He wanted to see her again, but he didn't know if she would allow him to. He was never rejected by any woman, and he wasn't sure how he would handle it if he got rejected by the one woman who stood up to him.

That night that they had spent together was incredible. There was just something about her that he couldn't put his finger on. The touch of her skin, the smell of her hair, the taste of her pussy, the sounds of pleasure she made he fucked her, these were all things that had lingered on his mind on a daily basis. She had him mesmerized. All had he knew is that he needed a way to convince her that he needed her. This was more than just a sexual need; he somehow felt completed.

A knock on the door interrupted his thoughts, "Mr. Forrest, I apologize, but this young lady said she needed to speak with you urgently." Mrs. Humphrey moved aside, and there stood Cassandra. Blake stood up immediately, but something was wrong. Her face looked strained; her eyes looked red and puffy as though she were crying. He thanked Mrs. Humphrey how nodded and closed the door behind her, leaving them alone.

Blake made his way over to Cassandra. He wanted to take her in his arms and just hold her, but he held back. He took her hand gently and led her to the sofa.

"What's wrong?"

She couldn't even look him in the

eye. He did, however, see her tears falling onto her shaking hands. He tilted her head upwards so that their eyes could meet. There was so much pain there; he wanted to make it all go away.

She cleared her throat. "I'm sorry I just needed to clear my head. I'm not even sure how I ended up here. I forgot the documents that night... that we... I wondered if you still had them?" Her voice cracked as she tried to withhold a sob.

Blake stood up and got the envelope from his desk and placed them in her hands. "I am a man of my word. Everything is in here." His hand covered hers, and he looked her in the eyes. "Please tell me what's wrong. Maybe I can help."

"There's nothing you can do. There's nothing anyone could do." With that, Cassie just crumpled before him. He held her close as she cried. He could feel her tears soak through his shirt. He wondered what could have made this very ferocious woman break like this. Then he remembered what she said about her father being ill.

"Is your father ok?" he whispered

softly in her hair.

She shook her head. "The doctors said that there isn't anything they can do for him. They have given up on him," she said between sobs.

He held her until her sobs quieted. She pulled away slowly from his arms and reluctantly he released her.

"I'm so sorry. I don't know what came over me. I think I should leave."

She stood, and so did he. She attempted to walk towards the door, but her knees gave away beneath her. Blake caught her and held her close. He scooped her up in his arms and placed her on the sofa.

"Cassandra is everything ok? Do you need me to take you to the doctor?"

Her eyes fluttered open. "I'm fine. I'm just a bit tired that's all. I really should be going." She swung her legs off the sofa and sat up slowly.

"Dammit Cassandra, you can't even make it to the door." He was surprised at how upset he was, how possessive of her he became all of a sudden.

He breathed deeply and continued more calmly, "Did you have lunch?" She shook her head. "Let me order us something to eat and then you can leave ok? How does Chinese sound?" She smiled and nodded in his direction. He walked towards his desk and made the call his eyes never leaving her. He watched as she curled her legs under her nestled her head into her arm that was resting on the sofa and close her eyes. Blake's heart went out to her, and he knew that she was the one for him.

7

Cassie's eyes flew open. She sat up slowly as her eyes adjusted to the darkness. It took her a while to remember that she was in Blake's office. The only light was the one that was coming through the top blinds from the corridor outside. She looked around the office, and she saw Blake leaning back in his chair. She couldn't tell if he was asleep or awake. All she knew was that she had made a fool of herself, and she needed to get out of there.

Her hands searched the floor for her shoes that were no longer on her feet. She slipped them on and then grabbed her keys and the envelope that was on the coffee table next to the sofa. She stood up slowly and as quietly as she could, she headed towards the door.

"You weren't planning on leaving without saying goodbye were you?" Blake's voice was husky and sounded so sexy at the same time.

Cassie spun around to face him, "I... I.. just didn't want to wake you."

He stood up and walked towards her, "Are you ok?" He stood in front of her and his finger trailed the side of her face.

"I'm ok; I just needed to get some rest. Thank you."

"But you haven't eaten. The food is here; all I need to do is reheat it. When I realized you were sleeping, I didn't want to wake you."

"Maybe you should have, what time is it?"

"It's around 11 pm," Blake said.

"What?? You should have awoken me. My sister will be worried. I need to leave." She walked away from Blake, and her hand reached for the doorknob, but Blake was faster. He turned her to face him, pinning her against the door.

"I spoke with Sam. I told her that you came to me with a business proposal regarding raising funds for the motel. I told her were would be running a bit late."

"Sam bought that?"

"Well, if she didn't she did not oppose." His hands rested comfortably on her hips and Cassie could feel that sudden urge to have him once more in her pussy. "Stay and have a late dinner. I promise I'll be good...if you want me to be." Cassie nodded. Blake brushed his lips across hers before moving to turn on the light.

She blinked a few times as her eyes once again adjusted. She looked over at Blake; his blonde hair was tousled, his shirt sleeve was rolled exposing his muscular arms, and he had the quaintest smile on his lips she had ever seen.

"There's a bathroom through that door if you want to freshen up a bit," he said as he pointed to the door on his left. "I'll start to reheat."

When Cassie returned from the bathroom, the office smelled heavenly. She was happy she decided to stay and eat, she was famished. Her tummy was growling so loudly she wondered if Blake heard it. If he did, he didn't say anything.

"Dinner is served," Blake said as he placed two plates of food at his desk. There was fried rice, chow mein, sweet and sour pork and stuffed dumplings.

"I'm not sure if I'll be able to eat all of this," Cassie said, as she sat down to eat.

"That's ok, eat what you can. I just want you to eat." He smiled at her as he dug into his food.

Cassie ate a bit of everything that was on her plate when she was finished she pushed her plate away.

"Are you finished?" She nodded and watched as Blake took the plates to the little kitchenette.

"Do you need help?" she asked, raising her voice a bit to ensure that he heard her.

"No, I'm good. I can handle it in here."

A few minutes later Blake was back. This time, he stood in front of her, arms folded casually as he leaned against his desk. He was unable to mask the concern that was on his face.

"I am ok Blake; I just didn't realize

how tired I was. Everything has been so hectic lately." She lowered her eyes. She couldn't bear for him to see her like this.

"Where is your father now?" he asked quietly leaning towards her.

"He's at home. Sam and I decided that that's where we want him. These are his last days, but my father isn't going down without a fight." She couldn't help but smile at her last statement.

"If there is anything I can do…" Blake said, his voice trailing off.

"Thank you, but you have done more than enough." She looked down at her watch. "I think it's time for me to leave."

Blake took her hand in his and pulled her gently to her feet. "I don't want you to go. But I'm not going to force you to stay. You are no longer obligated to."

"Do you want to stay?" Cassie nodded. If she walked out that door, she knew she would be making a mistake. She needed to him. She needed to feel safe.

****

What the hell are you doing Blake? This woman is vulnerable right now do you really think that this is the best thing to do? Blake tried to silence the voices in his head, but it was hopeless.

"Cassandra," he started.

"Call me Cassie, everyone else does,"

"Ok Cassie, as much as I want you to stay I don't know if it's the right thing to do, with everything that you have been going through."

"What do you mean?" she said, her brown eyes looking into his for answers.

"It means I like to play rough, and I don't want to hurt you. I also don't want you to regret it the next day, although I've never had a complaint before."

"Are you saying that I don't know what I want? You asked if I wanted to stay and I said yes, what is the issue?" The fire was back in her eyes again, and he couldn't help but chuckle.

"I just want to make sure that you know what you are getting into. The other night wasn't as rough as I usually go. It's a lot rougher than that."

"I'm a big girl, and I can handle it. I know what I want and if it means getting my brains fucked out so that I can get my bearings I'm willing to try anything. You turned on something in me the other night and since then I can't turn it back off."

"I know what you mean. I feel the same way about you. I just don't want you to get hurt."

"Well teach me; why don't you teach me?"

Blake thought about it for a moment. Never before has he set boundaries in the bedroom. He never needed to because women were always willing and at his disposal, but Cassie was different. He didn't even look at Andrea anymore as he used to. Even Albert asked him if he was sick because he was home almost every day and if he wasn't home he was working late at the office.

He walked over to the sofa and sat, patting his lap for Cassie to sit on him. She sat on him and wrapped her arms around his neck. He kissed her neck, and he felt her respond to him.

"We have to have some ground rules first,' he said in between kissing her neck

"Like what?" she moaned softly.

"Well, if this is going to work you are going to have to be totally submissive to me, no one else, ok?" She nodded as she massaged his head with her fingertips. He didn't know how much longer he could talk. His arousal was already busting and his zipper.

"Next if at any time you want to stop just say, uncle. That way I would know to back off."

"Anything else?" she asked slyly as her fingers maneuvered his cock from his pants.

"You need to trust me fully. Can you do that?"

Cassie nodded, slid between his legs and placed her mouth on his cock.

****

Cassie tasted the precum that was already on the tip of his cock. She wasn't sure if she would be able to put the entire thing in her mouth, but she sure as hell was going to try.

She gripped his cock firmly in one hand as her tongue teased the swollen head of his cock. As it throbbed in her mouth uncontrollably Cassie smiled, knowing that she could have an effect on a man such as Blake. She licked his shaft as her hands pumped him.

His groans were like music to her ears. She moved her mouth and slowly began to swallow him. The further she went down, the louder his groans got. Just don't gag, she begged herself. When his cock was three-quarters in her mouth, she used her hand to stimulate the rest of his cock.

His hands pushed her head further onto his cock as he fucked her mouth, hard. He held her head in place as he took full advantage of the fact that she wasn't protesting. She felt his cock hit the back of her throat, and she willed herself not to gag or vomit for that matter considering the fact that she had just eaten. She heard Blake groan hoarsely before she felt his liquids run down the back of her throat. He shuddered, making sure that every last bit was emptied before releasing her head. She swallowed the last of him and smiled at him, which he returned.

"Get out of those clothes," he commanded.

Cassie couldn't get out of her clothes fast enough. She watched as he tugged at his tie. When he got it off, he tied her hands behind her back and leaned her against his desk. She looked over her shoulder and watched as he quickly removed his clothes and put on a condom.

He came close to her and whispered in her ear, his cock fitting snug between her ass cheeks, "I won't be as gentle as I was before."

Without further warning, Blake rammed his huge cock into her pussy making scream out. She was certain that if there was anybody still left in the building they heard her.

He held on to her hands as he fucked her hard, her thighs bouncing roughly against the edge of his desk. He gently wrapped her long hair around his wrist, pulling her head up slightly which cause her ass to raise more towards him causing him to fuck her even more deeply.

She wanted to hold him as he fucked her, but she was tied. To wrap her legs around him to see the animalistic way he watched her as his cock invaded her most private areas. After the day she had this is just what she needed, rough sex never hurt anyone did it?

He moved her from the table, "Bend

over, straight as far as you can go." She obediently did as she was told. Blake opened her legs and found her clit as he thrust his cock back into her aching pussy.

She was feeling as though her legs would soon give out on her. She was reaching her peak, and she knew he was too. His thrust became harder and faster. She let out a torments scream as she released over his cock and a few thrusts later he reached his climax.

Without giving her a chance to catch her breath Blake said, "It's time to go. We'll finish this at the apartment."

8

Cassie glanced at her watch nervously. Blake was an hour late. He told her to be on time, and he wasn't. She didn't know anyone here. These were all high-class persons with real large estates who owned their own islands. But he said he needed a date and she was the most gorgeous woman that he knew so here she was.

She looked nervously at the door as she sipped from the glass of champagne that was in her hand.

A pair of arms wrapped themselves around her waist, "Why hello there beautiful." A familiar voice said from behind her.

Cassie turned around, and there stood face to face with Dean Jackson. She stepped away from him and turned to walk away. She had nothing to say to him. After she had wasted all that time and energy and it amounted to nothing. He grabbed her and pulled her back.

"Hey," Cassie said as she tripped over her gown and she almost fell but another pair of arms held her. This time, it was Blake's voice she heard.

"Is he bothering you?" Blake asked his voice tense.

"I wasn't bothering her. We are old friends. I just wanted to say hi," Dean said coldly.

Blake's eyes turned cold, "I wasn't speaking to you," he said as he put himself between Cassie and Dean, "I was speaking to the lady."

Blake looked as though he was ready to fight, and so did Dean. Both men were about the same muscular build, so it could go either way.

"Blake I'm fine now," Cassie said, tugging slightly on his arm. "Come on he's not worth it."

As they turned to walk away, Dean

muttered, "Bitch," a bit louder than he would have liked. Before Cassie could do anything, Blake's fist had already connected with Dean's face. Dean keeled over, holding his nose, blood seeping through his fingers. Blake grabbed Cassie roughly. "Let's go." Without saying another word, they left the building.

"What the hell is wrong with you?" Cassie glared at Blake as they reached the car park. "I could have taken care of myself."

"From where I was standing if I didn't get there when I did, you would have been flat on your face."

"You didn't have to hit him you know," Cassie almost screamed at him.

"Why not? When I arrived his hands were all over you." Was that jealousy Cassie detected in his voice? "And why are you so concerned about him anyway, or do you enjoy strange people wrapping their arms around you?"

Why did you care Cassie? It serves Dean right after everything he put you through you should be thrilled? But she wasn't; Dean's touch brought back so many memories that it made her heart sink.

"So are you going to answer me?"

"Why should I? My private affairs are my own."

Blake stepped towards her and kissed her hard. "You silly woman don't you see how upset I am that some other man had his arms around you? He's lucky that all he got was a broken nose," he said behind clenched teeth.

Cassie looked him in the eyes, "Can we at least sit? My feet are killing me in these shoes."

Blake took her hand, and together they walked towards his car. He opened her side and let her in before hurrying to the other side to get in himself. He put on the engine and warmth filled the car.

"Well?" Blake looked at her expectantly.

"He was my fiancé," she said. Blake raised his eyebrow, and she continued, "Well, my ex-fiancé."

He continued to look at her so once again she continued, "There's nothing to tell really. We had a pretty decent relationship. Like every relationship we had our ups and downs, but we always respected each other and what our relationship stood for. Until one day he left his phone at my apartment, and it rang. I answered it as I had done so many times before." Cassie could feel the tears coming on, but she continued, "It was his wife. She had a private investigator follow her husband when he went away on business trips, and that is where she found me. He also had two girls at home. I felt like such a fool. How could I have fallen in love with a married man? How could I not see the signs?"

Blake reached over and held her hand, bringing it up to his lips. "He was just good at what he did."

"But for two years? I knew that he traveled because his company was trying to open another franchise but not once did I think he was going home to his family when he left me. It took me almost a year to get over him. I didn't even leave my apartment. I just shut the world out."

"In my opinion, he needs more than just a broken nose. If you say the word, I could have it arranged for you."

Cassie looked into Blake's eyes searching it to see if he was serious but his eyes gave nothing away.

She sighed. "Nah, it's ok. I think I'll be ok. It's been three years. I didn't expect to see him there tonight. It brought up so many feelings of anger, hurt and pain. I just feel overwhelmed. But it will pass...hopefully."

Blake leaned forward and kissed her gently. She returned his kiss loving the feeling of his lips on hers as his tongue caressed the inside of her mouth. Her hands reached up to run her fingers through his hair. He lifted her up gently, and Cassie carefully crossed over to the driver's seat and sat on his lap straddling him. He lifted her gown and caressed her rounded ass before sticking his two fingers into her pussy. She quickly found unbuckled his belt and unzipped his pants. He lifted himself so that she could pull out his cock with ease. Her phone began to ring.

She reached over to her handbag, but Blake stopped her. "Let it go to voicemail. Please don't stop." Cassie was a bit hesitant, but she let it go to voice message.

Blake moved her panties aside, and she sat on his cock. He held on to her ass and moved her up and down as she rode him enjoying the fullness of him. Cassie unclasped the back of her dress pushing it down exposing her breasts to Blake, who hungrily took them in his mouth. The windows of the car became fogged, and the car became a sauna, but neither of them seemed to care. Cassie phone rang again, but she didn't want to answer it, she wanted to stay on Blake's cock. When it rang a third time, Cassie hopped off Blake, who protested and looked at the caller id. It was Sam. Cassie answered quickly her heart is pounding in her chest.

"Sam, what is it?" She said as calmly as she could as she slid into the passenger seat.

"It's Dad."

9

Blake watched as a wave of horror swept over Cassie's face. She hung up the phone and by the expression on her face, he knew something was wrong.

"What's wrong?"

"It's my father. He's been taken to the St. John's Memorial Hospital."

"Oh fuck, Cassie I'm sorry I should have let you answer your phone." Blake, you are such an ass. You knew her father was sick; you should have let her answer the phone. Blake quickly fixed his clothing and Cassie did the same.

The trip to the hospital was a quiet and intense one. Blake watched over in

Cassie's direction. Her head was against the window, and she was looking outside. He reached over and squeezed her hand, but she didn't respond, she just kept looking out the window. He knew that she would be expecting the worst on arrival at the hospital, and he also knew that she was the older sister, and she would want to be stronger for her younger sister.

Blake dropped Cassie at the entrance and told her that he'd be in soon enough. He found a parking space not too far from the entrance. He parked the car and headed quickly inside to find Cassie.

At the front desk, he asked for her, and the nurse directed him to the room. What he saw in the corridor tugged at his heart and made him stop in his tracks. Sam was being restrained by Cassie and a nurse. She was screaming and shouting. Blake couldn't hear what Cassie was saying, but by the loving way she stroked her sister's face she knew she was trying to calm her down.

Blake watched as a doctor and two nurses emerged from a closed room.

They chatted with Cassie and Sam for a bit before leaving. Sam shrieked like a wounded animal before collapsing into Cassie's arms. Blake rushed over them.

"Here, let me," he said as he gently picked up Sam and placed her on one of the couches. Cassie sat next to her. She lifted Sam's head and placed it on her lap. Blake stepped away and watched in awe as Cassie cradled Sam in her arms, comforting her. She looked down at Sam and Blake knew that she had to be strong for her. He knew that after her last episode at his office that she was not going to have another breakdown in front of him and definitely not in front of Sam.

She watched as Sam twitched beneath her and her eyes fluttered open. "Sam let's go home."

"I don't want to go home. I want to stay here." Sam sounded like a very defiant five-year-old.

"Sam hun, we can't do anything more tonight and staying here is not going to help either one of us."

Sam finally agreed, and Cassie turned to Blake. "Can you give us a ride home please?" Blake nodded.

Sam, with the support of Cassie, headed out of the hospital with Blake bringing up the rear.

****

Sam insisted that she sleep in her father's bedroom tonight and Cassie couldn't oppose her. Even though they knew that their father was dying, nothing actually prepared them for his death. She sighed as she closed the door to her father's bedroom. Sam was finally asleep. It was irresponsible of her not to answer her phone. She should have been there for Sam.

Cassie walked out into the small living room area, and she was surprised to see Blake sitting on the sofa.

"I thought you left?"

"Why would I?"

Great just what she needed, company. "I'm sorry Blake, but I'm not in the mood for company."

"Well, I'm sorry Cassie, but I'm not leaving at least not tonight. You may need me." He stood up and walked over to her, "Let me be here for you."

She knew that there wasn't anything

she could say that would make him change his mind.

"Would you like a cup of tea?"

"Sure, why not?"

Blake followed Cassie into the kitchen. He sat by the small round table. Cassie felt a bit conscious about the condition of the hotel. She knew that Blake was accustomed to more expensive settings. She watched as he stretched his long legs to the side because they could not fit under the table.

"I'm sorry about the accommodations. We usually don't have guests."

"I'm quite ok. The accommodations are fine; it's the company that I'm worried about."

"I'm fine," Cassie said, her back to him. She really wasn't, but it was in her personality to always be strong and never show any sign of weakness. "You never did tell me why you were late tonight."

"I had a late meeting at the office that went over time. I would have called your cell, but then I realized that I only had your office number." She heard him chuckle to himself.

As she was taking down the teacups from the cupboard one slipped and fell, shattering to pieces on the ground. She swore under here breath.

"Do you need help?"

"I'm fine," she snapped at Blake. She really didn't mean to. She got the scope and broom from the cupboard. She picked up all the big pieces and tossed them into the trash. It was just her luck that one of the pieces cut her finger, and she cried out. The blood trickled down her finger.

Blake was at her side at once. Cassie just melted in his arms. He rocked her like a baby and she gripped him close. He didn't seem to care that she was bleeding all over him. He held her as though she was the last person on earth. He was her safe haven, and she hoped that he would always be.

****

Monty was retiring and today his father was announcing who was going to replace him. After having a heart attack, Monty thought it wise to live out the rest of his life doing all the things he had planned to do with his wife. He worked hard, gave it his all now it was his time to hang up the cape.

Blake worked his ass off to help his father increase the profits of the company when he came on board. He knew that even though his father didn't like some of his tactics he couldn't doubt that he was one of the best that there was in his field.

No one knew who the candidate would be. If Monty knew he sure as hell wasn't talking. Blake walked into the conference room, and his eyes met that of Ridge, who smirked at him. He muttered something to the people around him who laughed.

When Rick and month entered to room the room became silent. They took their seats. They whispered something to each other before Rick stood to address the room.

"As you all know it is with a heavy heart that I say, Monty is leaving us. He has not only been a great friend but a true colleague. He has been with this company from day one and though there were many times when he could have backed out he didn't. He stood by my side helping me make this company what it is today."

A round of applause filled the room, and one or two persons whistled in agreement. Rick put up his hand indicating that he would like to continue speaking.

"We thought long and hard about who we should put in his place. It is never easy to move from one rung of the ladder to the next. It takes time and dedication to learn what it means to be a leader and how to clean up mistakes after they have been made. We needed someone with the skill, the drive, and the competitiveness to help take this company to the next level."

Everyone watched as Monty stood by the door, opened it and in walked his new replacement. All the blood from Blake's face disappeared. Rick continued, "Without further ado, I would like to welcome Mr. Dean Jackson as the new partner of our firm."

10

Dammit!!! Blake slammed the door as he entered his office. He flung his jacket on the sofa and sat behind his desk. He ran his fingers through his blonde hair and exhaled deeply.

What the hell was his father thinking about hiring outside help to run the company? He was his son for Christ's sake. He knew that company like the back of his hand and his father just gave it away. Not only did he give it away, but to Dean Jackson, Cassie's ex-fiancé. Dean was going to go for the jugular and Blake knew it.

There was a knock on the door which jolted Blake from his train of thought. Monty walked through the door, "I couldn't help but notice some tension between you and Dean."

Blake rubbed his temples and looked at Monty as he sat in the chair opposite to him. "I really screwed up, Monty. Dean and I had a little altercation a few weeks ago. Now it's come back to bite me in the ass."

"What do you mean by altercation?" Monty leaned back in his seat, rubbing his chin thoughtfully.

"I broke his nose kind of altercation."

Monty let out a slow whistle. As Blake started to speak to defend himself, Monty put up a hand. "Although I know that you are a hot head, I'm going to ask you three questions. Did he deserve it?" Blake nodded. "Is she worth it?" He nodded once more, and he could see a smile lingering on Monty's lips, "And last but not least what are you going to do about this situation?"

"I have no idea. But I might as well start somewhere." Blake stood up, got his jacket and nodded in Monty's direction. He was going to the big man himself, Rick Forrest.

****

Sam sat on the kitchen counter while Cassie made them dinner, fried eggs, toast, and tea. It was all they had in the fridge since the past few days they hadn't had time to run to the grocery in between preparing for their father's funeral. When finished, they both sat and ate quietly.

Cassie knew that they had some tough decisions to make even though they just buried their father. They needed money to repair the building since in the past few years no major repairs had been made, just a lot of patch jobs. She definitely wasn't going to sell the property after what she had done to keep it. The tenants here are like family, and now that her father was gone, she felt it was her responsibility to look out for them.

She looked over at Sam. She had changed so much in the past few days. If she wasn't crying, she was sleeping. She didn't eat much, and she just locked herself away in their father's room. Cassie sighed. She wished her mother was here; she could really use her support right now. She always knew the right things to say, and when all else failed, she would make a chocolate cake.

After dinner, Cassie washed up the dishes while Sam retreated to their father's room. Blake wasn't at her father's funeral, and she couldn't help feeling a bit disappointed. They weren't a couple or anything, but she just thought that with things going so well between them that he would have been there like he was at the hospital. She enjoyed being submissive in the bedroom, but she often wondered if that was all she'd ever be to him, a plaything.

She left the kitchen and headed towards her bathroom for a quick shower, then headed straight to bed. She crawled under the covers. Her mind tossed things back and forth making it difficult for her to sleep. She didn't know what time it was until she checked the clock on her nightstand. It said 1 am. Sigh. She needed to sleep. If she didn't get enough sleep, she would walk around like a zombie, and she couldn't have that. She felt as though she now needed to be able to function for two persons since Sam was hardly functioning. Because of her father's, she was able to convince the administrators at Sam's school to give her and extra month to finish her last two finals. She was almost at the end she couldn't fail now.

Cassie needed a release. She felt all the muscles in her back and shoulders tense. She hadn't masturbated in a while, but it was worth a try. It was always a good way to relax. Maybe it would knock her out. She got up, locked her door and removed her clothing.

She sat on her bed with her knees bent under her ass and her legs wide open. She pictured Blake was behind her as she gently kneaded her breasts picturing that he was the one touching her. She closed her eyes and rolled her head slightly to the side as she thought about him trailing light kisses down her neck.

She pinched her nipples and moaned, then squeezed her breasts tightly. She flicked her nipples until they were swollen. She bent her head and brought each nipple to her mouth, tasting herself, wishing it were Blake's mouth on her.

She allowed one hand to trail down between her wet legs. She passed her finger over her slit before opening it and finding her clit. She could already feel a heat come over her. She rubbed her clit slowly, allowing the feelings to run through her body. She pressed her fingers on her entranced and just patted herself, not wanting to enter just yet.

She moved her fingers to her lips, sucking her juices off each one before massaging her breasts once more adding more pressure. She roamed her body with her fingers using light and heavy pressure on her arms, her legs, her ass. She could feel her pussy throbbing, but she wanted to see how long she could hold out for.

She lay back on her bed and bent her knees and opened her legs as far as they would allow. With one hand she opened her pussy lips and with the other she explored it. She stuck two fingers in her slit and fucked herself. She pumped in and out, in and out. Her other hand was busy with her clit, increasing the pressure every time her fingers entered her.

She stifled her screams as she reached her climax. Panting, she removed her fingers from her dripping pussy and slowly let her legs down. Her bed was now covered with her sweat and her cum, but she was way too tired now to change her sheets. She hugged her pillow and found a part of the bed that wasn't drenched, and there she drifted off to sleep.

11

With her hands bound over her head, she was once more captive to whatever Blake wanted to do with her as she lay naked on her bed. She had been a bit startled to see Blake outside her apartment at 2 am but she was thrilled that he had come since he had been scarce for the past two weeks. She had to admit that she was starting to miss him. But tonight he was different. He seemed more intense, more withdrawn.

Cassie trembled as she watched Blake remove his clothing. His cock was already engorged, and she could feel her pussy throbbing with anticipation. Blake wiggled between her legs and slowly opened the folds of her wet pussy with his fingers. A soft moan escaped her lips.

He found her clit and gently rubbed it between his fingers. He allowed his fingers pass gently over her entrance though never penetrating her. Cassie groaned gently as his pace not only increased but so did the pressure. She could feel the sensations running from her pussy right down to her legs.

The more he rubbed, the more her pleasure increased and the louder her groans became. She was lucky that Sam decided to spend the night at a friend's house, or she would have some explaining to do the following morning.

Blake buried his head in her pussy while his fingers continued the assault on her clit. If he wasn't holding onto her hips, Cassie knew that she would have been wiggling all over the bed. He slid his fingers into her wetness and moved them slowly into her warmth.

Her nipples were hard and taunt, and they need attention. She could feel her body heat rising fast. Even though her pussy was getting well-deserved attention, she couldn't help but feel frustrated. She needed Blake touch every inch of her, satisfy every inch of her.

Without any warning Blake squeezed her clit, making her cry out sending mixed signals of pain and pleasure through her body. He did it, again and again, heightening her arousal more than it ever was. Her pussy was pulsing, and she wanted to cum, she needed to. Her clit felt bruised, but the sensation was amazing.

"I need to cum," Cassie whimpered.

"Not yet," Blake said in a very stern voice.

He got up and left the bedroom, leaving her more frustrated than ever. Time seemed to be standing. It seemed as though it was forever till he reentered the room.

Her eagerness began to build once more as Blake lowered his body on top of her. He opened her legs and thrust his cock into her forcefully making tears come to her eyes. With every thrust, his cock buried itself deeper into her pussy.

Cassie wrapped her hands around the iron bars of the bedpost to make sure that her head doesn't bounce into it. Blake lifted her ass from the bed and wrapped her legs around his hips as he continued to pound her. His hands found her clit once more, and she knew that she was spiraling out of control.

The air in the room seemed as though it was all gone and it got harder and harder to breath. Her chest was pounding; the bed was covered with her sweat and juices.

She couldn't control it anymore. She needed her release. She felt her pussy clench tightly around his cock before exploding all over him. That didn't stop Blake he continued to fuck her hard and assault her clit, making her cum over and over again.

Just when she thought she couldn't take anymore, Blake thrust deep into her, letting out a low grunt as he erupted. She lowered her legs onto the bed and Blake collapsed onto her. He didn't take his cock out of her immediately. He just lay there as though he was too tired to do anything else.

After a few moments, he disconnected them and slowly untied Cassie's hands. His lips brushed hers gently as he cradled her in his arms.

"What's wrong babe?" Cassie asked as she stroked Blake's face gingerly.

"Nothing."

Cassie turned her head so that she could look directly into his eyes. He seemed troubled. He unwrapped himself from her and sat on the edge of the bed, allowing his feet to touch the floor.

Cassie winced as she came up behind him. She tried to ignore the pain as she wrapped her hands around his waist, pressing her breasts on his back. "Come on Blake, I know something's wrong, why don't you just tell me what it is?"

He removed her hands slowly and got up very confident in the fact that he was naked. He found his boxers where he dropped them and put it on followed by his pants. Cassie wrapped herself in the sheet and sat up, looking at him concerned.

Blake looked over at her, and she raised her eyebrows. He sighed, "We got a new partner at our firm."

"And is that such a bad thing?"

"No, not unless you broke the guy's nose."

Cassie's eyes opened wide. "You've

got to be kidding me, Dean!? Your father hired Dean!?"

"Yup, and he's been making my life a living hell," Blake said through clenched teeth.

"Well, have you spoken to your father about it?"

"I tried, but as usual, it's always my fault. Nothing I do is ever going to please that man. He said life is about facing challenges and overcoming them, and then he got a phone call, and that was the end of our conversation."

"Is there anything I can do to help?"

"No, I guess I have to figure this one out on my own." He sat next to her and placed his arm on her legs, and she winced. This time, he noticed.

"Cassie, are you ok?"

"Yes, I'm fine. Nothing a nice long bath wouldn't cure."

He took her once again in her arms this time more gently. "I'm so sorry I took it out on you what a fool I was. I didn't mean to hurt you."

"I know you didn't," Cassie said as she kissed him gently on the cheek.

"I'm sorry that I have to fuck and run," Blake said as he kissed her forehead and stood up, "But I have an early meeting." He grabbed his shirt and put it on. "I can let myself out ok?" Blake gave her one last kiss on her forehead before letting himself out.

Cassie knew that she should be reminiscing about the time that she just spent with Blake, but Dean seemed to be causing trouble for Blake, and she wasn't going to have that. She wasn't the clueless girl he thought she was, and that could be used to her advantage. Cassie closed her eyes and smiled as she came up with a plan to get rid of Dean.

****

Cassie walked into the bar confidently. She knew she was late, and she didn't care. She wanted Dean to see her enter, and he wanted him to know that she would no longer abide by her rules.

When she called him earlier, he said that he was waiting for her call and if she wanted to discuss anything else that she would have to meet him at the bar at 7 pm, and she knew which one, after that the line went dead.

Cassie took her time to get dressed tonight. She took extra care in the shower and made sure that everywhere was well trimmed and ready to be on display. She wore a red dress with an extra low v-line cut which exposed her full breasts and held her curved hips nicely. Below she wore thin lingerie matching undies.

She walked further into the bar and saw Dean give her a slight wave. There weren't many people in the bar, maybe because it was a weekday. Before heading in his direction, she stopped and bought herself a martini. Her nerves were a wreck, and she needed her head in the game.

She smiled sweetly as she slid into the booth with Dean. It was somewhat secluded in a dark corner of the bar. She remembered coming here many times with him. This is where their foreplay started, and it would end in one of their apartments. But they were no longer together. This wasn't a welcome visit.

"Hi, babe." He drooled over her, "So glad you could make it."

"I'm glad to be here." Cassie forced a smile, thankful that the darkness of the booth hid what her eyes really showed.

"So you wanted to talk to?" He reached over and ran his finger along her arm. It took everything within her not to flinch. Just let him have his way. After tonight, he would no longer be a bother.

"Yes, why did you take the job at Forrest Enterprises?" she asked, looking ng him straight in the eye.

"I only took it because I knew I would see you again: that and the fact that I can now control the man who broke my nose." Dean rubbed his nose subconsciously. "You don't belong with him. You belong with me." He leaned his head in and tried to nuzzle her neck but this time, she pulled away.

"Woah there cowboy," she said, trying to make light of the situation. "So what can I do so you could back off of Blake?"

"Hmm, so there's no beating around the bush with you is there? You take charge and all. I like this "new" you." Cassie felt one of his hands on her thigh, but still she looked into his eyes. "Well, there is something that you can do."

"Which is?"

"Oh come on baby do you really need me to say it?"

She gulped the rest of her drink and placed her glass on the table, "Yes, I really need you to say it. I just want to make sure that we are on the same page."

"I want to fuck you," he said as he gripped her leg tightly under the table and this time, she flinched, "I didn't get the chance to have one last rendezvous with you but it's better late than never right?"

"If I let you fuck me; would you leave Blake alone?"

"Sure, why not, after all, he was trying to defend his lady's honor."

"Ok, so where do you want to do this?"

"Alicia's bed and breakfast. Do you know where it is?"

Cassie nodded.

"I'm assuming that you came here with your own vehicle?"

She nodded again.

"Good, I'll see you there in a few minutes."

Cassie got out of the booth followed by Dean. She needed to get that bed and breakfast before Dean.

12

Cassie sped down the highway hoping that she didn't see any police officers. Once parked, she did a quick surveillance of the car park. Good Dean wasn't there yet. Cassie grabbed the bags in the passenger's seat and hurried inside.

She walked up to the clerk, a pleasant looking older woman with the name tag, Eddie.

"Hi, I would like to have a room for the night please."

"Sure honey. Just you or are you expecting company?"

"Just me. I just need a night to hide away for a bit."

Just then Dean walked in.

"Oh shit," Cassie muttered.

The older woman looked over at Dean then at Cassie. "Is he the reason why you are hiding out?"

Cassie nodded. Eddie handed her the room key and directions. "Are you sure you're going to be ok?"

Cassie nodded and smiled politely leaving Eddie to tend to the next customer.

"Hey." She heard Dean's call, but she just walked faster. Panting, he caught her by the arm, and she pulled away violently enough for a few passersby to notice.

"What is your problem?" he hissed at her.

"Nothing," she said breezily.

He pushed her against the wall. "You better not be playing me bitch."

Cassie rolled her eyes and said softly, "Why would I drive all the way out here to play you? Look, I have something in my bag that I would like to try on for you ok? Meet me in my room in half an hour ok?"

Dean backed away slowly and nodded. Cassie adjusted her dress; she looked around slowly, and she saw the elderly clerk looking at her with concern. She flashed a smile to let her know that everything would be ok.

Cassie found her room and put on the lingerie that she bought. Nothing too fancy though a simply short laced gown with a matching pair of panties. She made sure that everything was set before she sat on the bed and turned on the television as she awaited her guest.

The room had one queen sized bed, a small television on a small table and one two seat sofa and a coffee table with a small bouquet of flowers. The bathroom was small, just good enough for one person, at least, they had hot and cold water.

There was a knock on the door, she got up and peered through the peep whole, sure enough, it was Dean.

She opened the door slightly the chain- hook was still attached to the door.

"Yes?" She batted her eyes playfully for him.

His eyes darted quickly over the gown, and he licked his lips. "Hmmm, so I see you like to play games. Just wait until I get inside. "

A couple passed by the door and Dean leaned closer so they wouldn't hear what he was telling her.

"Oh, are you teasing me? If you can get in yourself, then let the games begin!" She made sure that her voice was soft.

Cassie stepped away from the door and waited to see what Dean would do. She watched as his fingers tried to maneuver the chain, but he was unsuccessful. Just as she knew, he would have pressed his weight against the door, and the chain went flying.

She walked up to him and said softly, "I know how long you've waited for this and tonight there are no rules you are in charge." She pushed him and walked toward the bed. It wasn't long before Dean was on top of her ripping her clothes off.

After two hours of what had been the roughest sex she'd ever had, Cassie was exhausted, but she was almost at the finished line. When Dean fell asleep Cassie dressed quickly and collected her stuff, not forgetting the small camera that she had hidden in between the bouquet of flowers. She looked at Dean, who was sleeping so peacefully before opening the door and leaving.

****

When Sam asked her about the marks on her face the next morning, she simply said that she had been mugged. Sam asked if she made a police report, but she said those cases go unsolved anyway, and nothing of importance was stolen just some cash that she had on her.

Cassie looked over at Sam, her eyes filled with tears. "Oh Sam, I'm ok."

"I can't lose you to Cassie; I just can't."

"You won't Sam you won't," Cassie said as she rushed over to comfort her sister.

"Listen, Sam, I've got to go out for a bit would you be ok alone?"

Sam nodded, wiping her tears. As much as she wanted to stay and console Sam, she had bigger fish to fry.

Cassie walked into Forrest Enterprises like a woman on a mission. Dressed in a navy blue pants suit with black stilettos and a black briefcase she looked as though she belonged in the building.

She asked the receptionist where she could find Dean Jackson's office. When she got directions, she signed in and was given a visitor's badge. One her way to the elevators she saw Blake and she flashed him a smile. Luckily for her he was engaged in a group conversation with what looked like very important clients.

Cassie reached her destination, and she asked his secretary if he was in. That was all Cassie needed to know. She smiled politely and headed to his office, despite her protests.

She opened the door, and there was Dean, sitting by his table in what appeared to be a meeting.

He looked at her and even though she knew he was upset about the intrusion he forced a smile for his guests. He looked sternly at his secretary who was just behind Cassie.

"I'm sorry, Sir," she fumbled, not sure what else she could say.

"I'm sure you are," he replied, looking at Cassie.

"Why Cassie so nice to see you," he said as he walked over to her. He grabbed her hand and pulled her to the other side of the room before smiling once more at the two people gathered around his desk.

"You had to interrupt me now? This couldn't wait?"

"No, it can't. After what happened last night I think we should talk," she said, raising her voice a bit.

Dean grimaced. He turned to the person by his desk and apologized for the intrusion. He asked them if they could please give him a few moments alone that he had an emergency that he needed to take care of. His secretary who was still there escorted them out and finally she and Dean were alone.

"God dammit Cassie do you know how important those clients were? What is it that it couldn't wait?"

"Well," she said as she looked through her purse in search of her phone. As she looked through it for what she was looking for she continued, "I want you to leave Forrest Enterprises and never return."

Dean laughed his eyes no longer happy, his tone now menacing, "And what makes you think that you have the authority to tell me what to do?"

"This," Cassie said, handing him the

phone. She watched as his face turned from menacing to shock, and she continued, "What you are looking at is a video clip of you, Dean Jackson, raping me, Cassie Wells. Notice how I closed the door, and then you knocked down the door to enter my room? Also, notice how I'm struggling with you yet still you tossed me around? It's a good thing makeup can disguise anything." She touched her face, which was still a bit sore.

"Also, do you remember a few weeks ago when you grabbed me at the function in front all of those people and then again at the bed and breakfast? So Dean you have only one choice. Pack your shit and leave or I carry this to the police and have your ass arrested. Now how would it look if Senator Jackson's one and only son gets arrested for murder? This year is an election year isn't it? I bet the media will have a field day with this one."

Dean smashed her phone against the wall, and Cassie laughed fiercely. "You really think that was the only copy? Please Dean how stupid do you think I am."

He came towards her, then stopped

short as if he had had an epiphany moment, "That's right, you don't want to make a scene in here do you? Or that would just be adding more wood to the fire. Well, Dean, it was nice speaking to you. I expect to hear that you've resigned by the end of the week. Make up some lame excuse." With that, Cassie turned on her heels and walked out his office, leaving a dumbfounded Dean to try to figure out what had just happened.

13

"So what were you doing at the office this week?" Blake asked as he looked at Cassie. Every time he passed his hand over her face she flinched. She said she fell in the bathroom, but instinct told him that she wasn't telling him the truth.

"I went to check an old colleague of mine. Is that a problem?"

"Did that old colleague happen to be Dean?"

Cassie looked him straight in the eye. "Yes, as a matter of fact it was? And I repeat is there a problem?"

"Of course, there's a problem," Blake

said, getting up from the sofa. He began to pace. "Especially since there's a rumor going around the office that something happened between the two of you. Did something happen between the two of you?"

Blake knew that more than just 'something' had happened since Dean resigned from the firm claiming that he got a better offer somewhere else. He knew that it was no coincidence that Cassie was in his office the same week that he resigned.

"Yes," Cassie said, still looking at him straight his eyes, her gaze not wavering.

"When we started this I made it quite clear that I am the only man that you are supposed to sleep with did I not? I'm assuming you had sex with him?"

Even though Blake knew the answer, he still cringed when she answered yes.

Blake exhaled deeply. He wanted to know more he needed to know more.

"You know that you disobeyed me right? It means one of two things. One that I tell you to leave and this right here and now.."

"No, you can't do that!!" Cassie said, looking at him with those big puppy dog eyes of hers.

Blake held up his hands for her to be quiet, which she did. "Or two you can be punished. But before I give you that chance of choosing I would like to hear exactly what happened, especially with your face and don't give me any cock and bull story about slipping in the bathroom. I'm no fool, Cassie. You either be straight with me now or you can leave now."

He watched as Cassie inhaled deeply and then told him exactly what happened. That she and Dean met at the bar, then they headed to the bed and breakfast. How she had hidden the camera in the flowers and told him one of her fantasies was to be held down while having sex which made it look so convincing that she was being raped. She went to the office and showed him the tape, telling him that he needed to leave, or she would expose him.

Blake sank into the sofa. Never would he have expected that from Cassie, but she had put herself in danger, and he didn't know how to deal with that.

"Cassie," he said firmly, "Don't you think I would have been able to handle

Dean on my own? Don't you think that I am capable of handling my own affairs? Why did you have to put yourself in danger? What if things had turned out differently? What if he had really hurt you then?"

Blake stood up and headed straight for the door. "Now is your time to make your choice, be punished or leave and we will end this right now." Cassie stayed right where she was, and Blake looked at her.

He went over to her and lifted her face towards his own. "I'll say this just once. You were spared this time, and it's only because I've grown fond of you. If you ever sleep with another man or even let another man touch you sexually it's off, you wouldn't even have a say in the matter. And if you ever, ever put yourself in that kind of danger again for me and something were to happen to you I would never forgive myself."

"Now strip, it's time to be punished."

****

Cassie held on to the back of the sofa for dear life. Blake commanded her to hold on and not to let go. She let go, and she was struck with his belt on her ass. Even though he rubbed it after striking the blow, it still hurt.

"After that story you just gave it appears that you like to play rough and all, this time, I didn't think that you were ready."

She turned her head to face him. "Don't look at me," he snapped, "keep your eyes on the ground." Cassie did as she was told. She had never seen Blake so bossy during sex, and she wasn't sure if she liked it.

"Ow," she cried as the belt connected with her skin.

"I asked you a question. Now is not time to think. Now is the time to listen to my commands and obey."

She nodded, here head still bowed.

"Did you like it when Dean fucked you?"

Even though Cassie though that she got over Dean she had to admit that feeling his cock in her was more pleasurable than she thought but would she admit that to Blake?

Cassie winced Blake struck her ass again with the belt.

"Why are you taking so long to

answer Cassie? Did you like it when Dean fucked you?"

"No," she said, hoping that she was convincing enough. She cringed as she thought her ass would get another blow but it didn't.

"Now how am I going to know that you will not run off again and get fucked by someone else?"

"I don't know?"

Smack. She felt her knees weaken. She almost let go to rub her ass, but then she would have received another blow.

"I didn't ask you a question. I was just talking out loud."

From the corner of her eye, she saw Blake come behind her with the belt still in hand, and she began to panic.

"Open your legs."

She did Blake took one of her legs and placed it on the back of the sofa.

"Cock your ass out as far as you can."

She did as she was told. Now her pussy and ass were exposed to him. He said nothing for a while, but she knew that he was taking her in with his eyes.

Blake took the belt and rubbed it on her pussy lips. He whispered in her ear, and he pinched her nipples hard, "The next time you think about putting another cock in MY pussy you'll think again."

Smack! This time, the belt made contact with her pussy. She fought back the tears. Her pussy was throbbing like never before. She wasn't sure if it was from the blow it just got or if it was from the excitement that she was feeling. The pain in her body was running between her nipples and her pussy. He tugged and pulled at her nipples until they were throbbing as much as her pussy.

Again and again, he hit her, never increasing in pressure, which she was happy for. She didn't know how much her legs; pussy or nipples could take or how much she could take for that matter. By now her pussy was wet, and Cassie was ready to feel Blake's cock in her. As though sensing her thoughts, Blake put down the belt and slowly but her leg down. He scooped her up and headed for the bedroom.

14

Blake knocked on the door to his father's office and peeked inside. He wasn't sure why he was being called in, but he hoped it had something to do with the replacement of Dean Jackson. His father waved him in, and he took a seat until his father had finished his conversation.

"So why have you summoned me?" Blake asked curiously.

"Well, you know we now have an opening for another CEO of our company." Rick looked at him straight in the eyes, "And I'm sorry to tell you this, but I gave the position to Ridge."

"What??" Blake jumped out of his

chair and leaned his hands on his father's table and looked him in the eye. He was furious. "After everything I have done in this company? After all the clients I secured you gave the position to Ridge?"

"Yes, I did," his father said calmly as he leaned back in his chair and pointed at Blake's seat which he reluctantly returned to. "You see Blake; you never could separate your business life from your social life. You really think I don't know about the people that you've fucked in here? You really don't think that after all the partying that you have done that you could just take leadership of this company? You think that your skeletons won't come out of the closet eventually? And where would that leave the company and the many people who depend on it? And what happened the other day with Dean, you think I don't know about that? We lost one of the best because you couldn't control one of your chicken heads or rather yourself since you were the one that struck the first blow. You still have a job here, and that is only because I promised your mother on her death bed that I would look out for you."

Blake went from furious to rage, but in spite of he stood up and calmly said, "Ever since I could remember I did everything in my power to please you. I went to all the schools you wanted me to. Did all the classes, even dated a few of your friends' daughters so that you could seal a business deal. But I realize now that it doesn't matter what I do, that you will never ever be proud of who I am, and I am ok with that. I'll send in my resignation letter, and it will be effective from today. I'll send in someone tomorrow to clean out the rest of my things in my office." Blake turned away and walked out of his father's office for the last time.

Blake pulled into the car park at the motel. He needed to see Cassie, but did she want to see him. Since being with her he hadn't been with anyone else, nor did he want to be with anyone else. This was the first time in his life where he didn't feel the burden of needed someone else's opinion of how he should live his life. As Blake Forrest, he had an image to uphold, but he no longer cared about that. He only wanted one woman, and that woman was Cassandra Wells.

Blake walked into the motel and saw Mack. "Hey is Cassie in?"

"Yeah, she's in the office. Go on in," Mack said as he waved him in.

Blake didn't remember seeing her car in the parking lot he wondered if it was at the mechanic.

Blake knocked on the door. "Come in."

He opened the door, and there was Cassie shuffling through papers.

"Hi," she said, giving him a brief smile before returning her attention back to the papers.

He took a seat opposite her and unbuttoned his jacket. He watched as a few strands of her long black hair fell over her face. Today she was more casual than usual. She had on a thin strapped vest which to his delight exposed her cleavage. He felt himself getting aroused and he knew it was time to concentrate on something else.

He cleared his throat. "I didn't see your car in the car park is it by the mechanic?"

"No, I sold it," she said still

thumbing through her papers.

"Why?" When he realized that she wasn't paying attention, he placed his hand on her papers which forced her to look up.

"What?" she said half annoyed, under her eyes, had bags as though she hadn't been sleeping well.

"Why did you sell the car?"

"Because I needed the money to do some repairs to the building. Daddy would usually have the building up to par with regulatory codes because he was sick for the past couple of years' things were left undone. I didn't know how bad things got until I came a few months ago." She removed the ponytail from her hair and let it fall across her shoulders.

"How can I help? It seems that I have some free time on my hands."

Cassie looked at him strangely. He then proceeded to tell her about what had happened in her father's office. He watched as Cassie looked mortified and she covered her mouth with her hands.

"Oh my God, I'm so sorry I was just trying to help you. I didn't know it would have caused more harm than good. I...."

"It wasn't your fault. Things happen. My father was never and an easy man to please, and it doesn't matter what I did he never was. So I'm no longer going to live by his rules but by my own. I hope that when I have children one day that I'll be a better father than he ever was."

Cassie smiled at him. "Hmmm, I didn't know that you wanted children. You don't seem the type."

"And what type do I seem like?"

Cassie blushed and looked down at her desk. "If I don't answer will I be punished?" She looked up at him through her long eyelashes.

Blake laughed heartily. "No you won't get punished, but I would like to know what type of person you think I am."

"Well," she said slowly, "you seem like the type of person who always wants to be in control and with children you can't "control" them. You guide them, you teach them, but never control them."

"But that's only in the bedroom. But yes, I guess at times I can be controlling outside of the bedroom at times, but maybe I need the help of someone who isn't afraid of telling me when to back off." He looked into her eyes, wondering what was going on inside of her head, wondering if she was feeling the same way that he was.

He stood up and went behind her chair and pulled her up to meet him, "I guess what I'm trying to say is I want something more than what we have in the bedroom. I don't want you to think I'm always like that. I can be a fun, romantic guy as well. I just like to keep things spiced up in the bedroom."

"I'm not sure if I want to be spanked for the rest of my life, though," Cassie said.

Blake chuckled, "Well, maybe we can save those for special occasions." He bent over and kissed her on the lips softly.

"Maybe, I need more convincing than that," Cassie smiled up at him. "How about becoming an investor in the motel? It would give you something to do while you think about your next move?"

"Going into business with a hardcore woman such as yourself makes me shiver. Do you remember the first deal that we made together?"

Cassie bent her head into his chest and groaned, "Please don't bring that up?"

"Why not? You are so cute when you're nervous."

Cassie laughed, then looked at him thoughtfully. "Do you really think the Mighty Blake Forrest can settle down with a commoner like me? We are from different worlds Blake."

Blake held her close. "The only world I'm concerned with is the one I'd be sharing with you."

This time, it was Cassie who reached up and pulled his head down to meet hers. They kissed passionately.

"Go lock the door," Cassie said. "And I'll clear the desk." Blake locked the door and watched in amazement as Cassie cleared the table with one swipe of her hand. She sat on the table, and he snuggled in between her legs.

"You know that's gonna be a bitch to clean up don't you?" he said, running his fingers along her arms.

"Yeah I know, but I also know you'll make it worthwhile."

AUTHOR'S NOTE

Readers: I want to expand a few of the stories to see where the characters can be explored further. If there are any of the stories that you would like to read more about again, I'd love to hear from you!

Visit my blog at http://www.jaelynnmccranie.com/

Join my newsletter for free exclusive previews
http://jaelynnmccranie.com/newsletter/

Follow me on Twitter at
http://www.twitter.com/jaelynnmccranie

Like my page on Facebook at
https://www.facebook.com/jaelynnmccranieauthor

Discover my books at major ebook retailers everywhere.